Baby Shopping

Taylor Sapp

Alphabet Publishing

Contents

Before You Read

1. In the future, will people be able to choose what their babies look like or act like?

2. What are the good sides of that? What are the downsides?

3. What features would your ideal baby have? What would they look like?

Baby Shopping

A husband and wife were at Best Baby, one of the most famous stores that sold designer babies. The store was full of 3D holograms of babies with different looks and abilities. There was a small thumbprint in front of each display and a button to choose either *boy* or *girl*. They both stopped to stare at a large sign that read

YOUR BEST BABY! YOUR BEST DNA! PERFECT GENETIC EDITING! 10 - YEAR GUARANTEE!

The wife looked at her husband. "It's all our own DNA?"

"That's correct!" A slick-haired salesman in a suit popped out of nowhere.

"The baby is you! We don't add anything! We take your best DNA to ensure the baby is healthy. We can also select characteristics that you both already have, like eye color, height, or certain other traits. Then we also have a number of special skills and abilities we can add in to make the baby smarter or stronger or taller! Please take a look around. I'm happy to help with any questions."

The husband and wife thanked the salesman and continued looking. First, they went to the Theme Packages Sections. Here there were babies with groups of different attributes and skills, from super eyesight to super intelligence to a bodybuilder's muscles.

The husband was looking at the *Sport* model. This little baby hologram was wearing a baseball hat and catching a baseball. The husband could imagine his son making the World Series playing for the New York Yankees!

If only they had the money. The prices were clearly meant for rich people, which they definitely were not!

The wife was shaking her head. "It's out of our budget, dear. Let's look for something a bit cheaper."

They headed for the Custom-Build-A-Baby Section. Here you could choose a baby with only a few enhanced abilities. There were three packages depending on how many features or abilities you wanted to add.

As the two were both teachers, the silver package was already going to be a bit of a stretch, but they could just manage it. So that's where they headed.

They stopped to look at the list of attributes:

Build-Your-Own-Baby

Choose from the list below to build the perfect baby!

I.   Silver: Choose 1

II.   Gold: Choose 2

III.   Platinum: Choose 3

athletic ability

artistic skills

math and science

physical size and strength

better health

business and negotiation skills

creative writing

musical ability

compassion and kindness

They both were discussing the various options when, clearly sensing the moment, the salesman popped up again in front of them, smiling.

"You can't go wrong with any choice!" the salesman said, "With your DNA samples, we can get your new little boy or girl by the end of the week! Or if you'd prefer a natural birth, we can implant the genome-edited embryo directly."

The wife grabbed her husband excitedly, "Let's do it, honey! I don't want to waste any more time!"

"Remember we're going to have to choose just one area to enhance our baby unless we want to sell our car and house!" he said

"I want a daughter who can play piano like a dream!" she said.

"And I want a son who can pitch for the Yankees," he said.

"We'll have to compromise. What about better health?" she asked.

Dad agreed. A child with good health would play sports better anyway. They couldn't agree on gender. The salesman said they could leave it to chance, just like a natural birth!

Dad shrugged and looked at the salesman. "OK, what's the next step?"

"Just enter both your thumbprints on the display and press the 'order now' button to confirm. Your DNA is collected, some papers to sign will print out and that's it!"

The husband and wife looked at each other and stepped up to the display and pressed the button.

Suddenly, the lights in the store started flashing. Loud, exciting music started playing!

"Well, how about that! It looks like you're our one-millionth order!"

"What does that mean?" The husband could barely hear over the noise.

In the salesman's office, they signed the paperwork as he explained their bonus. He went over the standard legal language, about how the baby would be created with their DNA, grown in a super-fast incubator at one of their nearby facilities, and delivered upon completion. No refunds or exchanges, unfortunately.

The salesman had a big smile! "You guys have no idea how lucky you are. As our one-millionth customer, you're the first to get our newest upgrade.

"Upgrade?" both parents asked simultaneously.

"I'd hate to spoil it; you'll see soon enough!"

Just five days later, their new baby girl was delivered to the house via White Glove Delivery along with a *Best Baby* matching stroller and portable crib.

Mom and Dad welcomed Baby into the house and stared at her perfect face. Both Mom and Dad were physically average in almost every way, which meant imperfections from Dad such as big ears and a big nose, and thin lips from Mom. But thanks to the process of combining DNA, only Dad and Mom's best traits were combined.

If anything, Baby might have had her mom's slightly large nose, but it actually helped her face stand out more. Dad's gene for hair loss was balanced by Mom's good genes. Mom desperately had wanted to pay for the stunning-blue-eyes gene from her favorite actress, but it was too expensive. Besides, they still didn't know what the mystery upgrade was.

As their wonderful Baby grew and became a beautiful young Daughter, she seemed perfect in almost every way to Mom and Dad. They couldn't figure out what the upgrade was. Until one day, when they discovered just how special their Daughter was.

Mom kept a cookie jar on the counter locked with a 3 number code. But somehow, their now 4-year-old Daughter kept opening it! Mom kept changing codes, but their Daughter kept getting in. It was when she sat her daughter down and asked her to guess the numbers in Mommy's mind that she realized just how special her Daughter was.

***

"Telepathy? You mean like reading minds?"

The salesman, a touch older and grayer and now celebrating sale number ten million, tried his best to hide his own mixed feelings.

"I told you it would be a big surprise! It's part of a new Psychic Powers Pack that the engineers are developing. Telepathy is just the start. Telekinesis, moving things with your mind, is next. They were working on mind control, but obviously that could be a bit dangerous! Just imagine giving your 3-year-old that power! It would be cookies for breakfast, lunch and dinner!"

"You don't think this kind of thing is going too far?"

"Look, my job is to sell the product I'm given. It's the people upstairs that make those kinds of decisions. If we can keep adding improvements to our product..."

"Is this telepathy removable?"

"Ask her."

"It's not," Daughter said.

***

In the early days, Mom and Dad were able to keep their Daughter from using her special ability. Because telepathy was an extremely expensive add-on, it was also rare. So the Daughter was the only telepath in her school or even the whole town. Of course, this gave her a huge advantage on tests and homework, and on understanding other kids. But it also came with its own frustrations.

"What's the point in reading minds if I can't change them?" Poor Daughter felt too often helpless about her ability, as it just allowed her to know too much! One day when she was 16, she came home crying. The guy she liked had asked her to the prom, but she could read his mind; he was only doing it to get close to one of her friends.

With little trouble, Daughter always got top grades, enough to get into a top-level university. She continued to keep her special ability a secret, and never used it to cheat. She learned everything herself. Her psychic abilities simply helped her understand better. She also did well at group work and presentations. She always gave teachers exactly what they wanted.

She became a therapist, one with an ability to understand her patients deeply. She specialized in helping families, especially moms and dads to get along, after helping her parents stay together and not get divorced. She became highly regarded and wealthy, and the author of several best-selling books on how to have a happy home.

Privately, the CIA used her skills to get information from bad guys. She never wanted to work for them full-time though.

***

When the time came, Daughter and her husband, Max (who was also enhanced with super intelligence and health and strength, but nothing extraordinary) found themselves in the same Best Baby, this time looking for the greatest and latest model. The same old salesman, now quite gray, never forgot about his lucky customer.

"You'll be sad to hear that the telepath feature is no longer offered, but we have made a lot of new improvements in the last 30 or so years..."

Many years later, three generations sat down for Christmas—grandparents, parents, and grandchildren—all together.

The daughter, now a mother, of course, knew what everything was, even though she tried to block it out. There were never any surprises for her.

And the grandchildren? The two perfect children, one boy and one girl, without any genetic or character flaws, sat perfectly content, playing with their gifts.

The Grandson had asked for a box of gears and computer chips. Now he was using his advanced engineering and electronics knowledge to make a personal robot.

The Granddaughter was busy having a conversation with her new puppy who was nervous about being away from her mom. Animal speech was still new, but not uncommon. Their parents tried to help them with their presents, but the grandchildren waved them off.

As their grandchildren shook their heads at their parents, the not-quite-as-evolved grandmother and grandfather couldn't help but smile just a little.

Glossary

a crib: a bed for babies and small children that has bars on the sides

an embryo: an unborn human at the earliest stages still in the mother's womb

the genome: the complete set of genes

a hologram: a three-dimensional image

an imperfection: mistakes, things that are wrong with something

to implant (*here*): place an egg or embryo in a woman's womb

incubator: a device that keeps eggs warm and safe

platinum: a precious metal like gold or silver

psychic: (here) special abilities that allow you to control things with your mind

slick: shiny

telekinesis: the ability to move things with your mind

telepathy: the ability to read minds

After You Read

1. Why do the mother and father go to Best Baby?

2. What does Best Baby do?

3. What limitations do the mother and father face?

4. What decision do they make for their baby?

5. What is special about their new baby?

6. What ways does Daughter use her abilities?

7. What are the benefits and drawbacks?

8. What abilities do the grandchildren have?

9. What would you do if you had the Daughter's abilitities?

10. If you could choose any genetic feature for your child, what would you choose? Why?

11. Do you think science will make any of the super abilities in the story possible in the future? Why or Why not?

12. What regulations or rules do you think there should be about children

13. Is being able to edit the DNA of a child a good thing or not?

Writing

Continue the story.

- What happens to the grandkids?

- How do their powers help or hurt them in the future?

- Do they run into any conflicts?

More Readers

AlphabetPublish.com/Book-Category/
Graded-Reader

www.ingramcontent.com/pod-product-compliance
Lightning Source LLC
Chambersburg PA
CBHW071953190726
48293CB00004B/1453